Dear Parent:
Your child's love of reading starts here!

Every child learns to read in a different way and at his or her own speed. Some go back and forth between reading levels and read favorite books again and again. Others read through each level in order. You can help your young reader improve and become more confident by encouraging his or her own interests and abilities. From books your child reads with you to the first books he or she reads alone, there are I Can Read Books for every stage of reading:

SHARED READING
Basic language, word repetition, and whimsical illustrations, ideal for sharing with your emergent reader

BEGINNING READING
Short sentences, familiar words, and simple concepts for children eager to read on their own

READING WITH HELP
Engaging stories, longer sentences, and language play for developing readers

READING ALONE
Complex plots, challenging vocabulary, and high-interest topics for the independent reader

ADVANCED READING
Short paragraphs, chapters, and exciting themes for the perfect bridge to chapter books

I Can Read Books have introduced children to the joy of reading since 1957. Featuring award-winning authors and illustrators and a fabulous cast of beloved characters, I Can Read Books set the standard for beginning readers.

A lifetime of discovery begins with the magical words "I Can Read!"

Visit www.icanread.com for information on enriching your child's reading experience.

For Nola Peterson, my
reading buddy
—J.O'C.

For Ally Muchnick, model
extraordinaire
—R.P.G.

For C., who made every
day very not dull and
often quite fancy indeed
—T.E.

I Can Read Book® is a trademark of HarperCollins Publishers.

Fancy Nancy: Fancy Day in Room 1-A   Text copyright © 2012 by Jane O'Connor   Illustrations copyright © 2012 by Robin Preiss Glasser   All rights reserved. Printed in the United States of America. No part of this book may be used or reproduced in any manner whatsoever without written permission except in the case of brief quotations embodied in critical articles and reviews. For information address HarperCollins Children's Books, a division of HarperCollins Publishers, 10 East 53rd Street, New York, NY 10022. www.icanread.com

Library of Congress Cataloging-in-Publication Data is available.
ISBN 978-0-06-208305-0 (trade bdg.) — ISBN 978-0-06-208304-3 (pbk.)

12 13 14 15 16   LP/WOR   10 9 8 7 6 5 4 3 2   ❖   First Edition

Fancy NANCY

Fancy Day in Room 1-A

by Jane O'Connor

cover illustration by Robin Preiss Glasser

interior illustrations by Ted Enik

HARPER

An Imprint of HarperCollinsPublishers

I am peering out the window
of my classroom.
(Peering is a fancy word for looking.)
It has rained all week.
We can't play outside.

Ms. Glass is reading a story.

Everybody looks glum and gloomy.

(That's a fancy way to say

we are in a bad mood.)

She puts down the book.

"Class, we need something fun

to look forward to," Ms. Glass says.

"Does anyone have ideas?"

We all sit and ponder.

That means we think hard.

Clara says,

"Let's go bowling."

Robert says,

"Let's go see a movie."

Ms. Glass says,

"Those are interesting ideas.

But let's think of

something to do in school."

At home

I ponder while I pick out

a dress for tomorrow.

I never feel glum or gloomy

in this fancy dress.

Being fancy is fun.

It makes me happy.

Ooh la la!

All of a sudden

I have an idea.

My pondering has paid off!

The next day at school I say,

"What if we have a fancy day?

We can wear fancy clothes

and eat fancy food

and use fancy manners!"

12

Lionel holds up his pinkie.

"Oh, darling," he says.

"You must try the baked worms!"

Ms. Glass looks stern.

That means now is not the time

to be silly.

"I think this is a great proposal,"
Ms. Glass says.

She explains that a proposal
is like an idea.

Everybody else likes my idea too,
even Lionel.

"Next Monday will be Fancy Day,"
Ms. Glass says.

"We can start preparing now."

We make fancy place mats.

We make fancy napkin rings
from pipe cleaners.

We also make fancy crowns.

Lionel makes the points on his crown

look like bloody shark teeth.

He is such a goofball!

At snack time we put napkins
on our laps.

We chew with our mouths shut.

When Robert burps,

he says, "Pardon me."

I teach everyone how to say

thank you in French.

"It's *merci*.

You say it like this:

mair-SEE."

That evening,

I tell my family about Fancy Day.

"It was my proposal.

That means it was all my idea!"

Over the weekend
Bree and I bake cupcakes
for Fancy Day.

On Sunday night

I look through my wardrobe.

That's fancy for all my clothes.

I find my most fancy dress.

I will also wear boas, bracelets,

tons of necklaces, lace gloves,

and sparkly clips in my hair.

I am fancy all the time,

so I must be super-duper fancy

on Fancy Day.

On Monday morning

I am stunned.

(That means surprised.)

Everyone looks so posh.

But where is Ms. Glass?

Why isn't she here yet?

All of a sudden Ms. Glass rushes in.

Her tooth broke this morning.

The dentist already fixed her up.

She is fine now.

But she is not fancy.

Ms. Glass looks startled.

(That means surprised,

only in a bad way.)

"Oh no!" she cries.

"I left all my fancy stuff at home!"

We tell Ms. Glass not to feel bad.

"You can have my clips," I say.

Bree offers her boa.

Everyone helps dress up Ms. Glass.

It is like playing with a giant doll.

In no time, she is super posh.

Soon it is party time.

Ms. Glass says,

"We must thank Nancy for Fancy Day."

The kids all lift their cups
of lemonade.

Everybody's pinkie is up.

But no one says thank you.

They all shout, *"Merci!"*

Fancy Nancy's Fancy Words

These are the fancy words in this book:

Glum and gloomy—in a bad mood

Merci—"thank you" in French (you say it like this: mair-SEE)

Peer—look

Ponder—think hard

Proposal—an idea

Startled—surprised in a bad way

Stern—not pleased

Stunned—surprised

Wardrobe—all my clothes